For Abby and Luca,
may you always chuckle

First published in 2010
by Walker Books Australia Pty Ltd
Locked Bag 22, Newtown
NSW 2042 Australia
www.walkerbooks.com.au

National Library of Australia
Cataloguing-in-Publication entry:

Johnstone, Matthew.
Harvey, the boy who couldn't fart / Matthew Johnstone.

ISBN: 978 1 921529 83 2 (hbk.)

For primary school age.
A823.4

The illustrations for this book
were created with digital media.
Typeset in Providence Sans
Printed and bound in China

10 9 8 7 6 5 4 3 2 1

Harvey, the Boy who Couldn't Fart

written and illustrated by
Matthew Johnstone

WALKER BOOKS
AND SUBSIDIARIES

LONDON • BOSTON • SYDNEY • AUCKLAND

There once was a boy called Harvey.
Harvey's life was pretty good except for one thing ...

No matter how hard Harvey tried,
he just couldn't fart.

NOTHING

Everyone else in Harvey's family
seemed to be quite good at it.
Rusty the dog did the
"silent but violent" types.

Harvey's brother, Max,
liked to fart in the bath.

"BUBBLES FROM BELOW!!"
he yelled with glee.

Harvey's sister, Pippa,
only farted when she
thought no one was around.

quack

Harvey's dad thought
he was being clever by
covering up a fart with
a cough, but it never
fooled Harvey.

cough!

WAAAAARRP!!

11

Harvey had caught his mum farting only once. It wasn't very impressive but it was one fart more than Harvey had ever done.

The biggest farter in Harvey's family was his grandad. He did the loudest "trouser trumpets" Harvey had ever heard.

FAAAAAWAAAA!!

pffft

13

And Harvey's friends were experts.
They loved to show off their
backfiring abilities.

Poor Harvey.

One day Harvey was feeling sorry for himself.

His grandad asked what the matter was.

"I can't fart," sighed Harvey.

"Well, I'm a bit deaf, I need glasses and I have false teeth; so you're really quite lucky," said Grandad.

Harvey thought Grandad had a point.

"But," said Grandad, "I may have a solution to your problem. Wait right here."

With that,
Grandad disappeared
into the garden shed
where he proceeded
to make a lot
of racket.

Grandad finally emerged looking triumphant.
He presented Harvey with the most unusual-looking
contraption made out of a piece of wire,
two rubber bands and an old washer.

"What is it?" asked Harvey.

"It's your very own farting machine," said Grandad.

Grandad then gave
Harvey a demonstration.

STEP 1: Wind the washer up
until the rubber bands are
nice and tight.

STEP 2: Holding onto the washer
firmly, place the farting machine
under your bottom, on a soft seat,
with the washer facing outwards.
Sit down and then let go of the
washer.
Note: For the best results try it
on a vinyl-covered seat.

STEP 3: Slowly lift your bottom and your farting machine will do the rest.

PAAAARRRrrr...

You can practise doing quick ones, slow ones or lots of little ones.

19

Harvey was the happiest
boy in town.
And he wanted
everyone to know it.

FAWAAAAAAARP!!!

He even went on to win a nice trophy.

THE REAR END